# Every Day Is a HOLIDAY

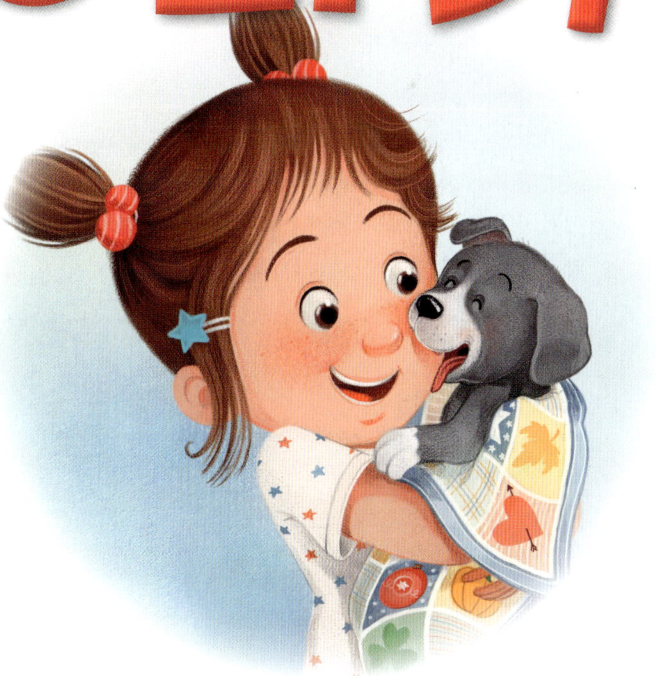

by Greg Kincaid

New York Times bestselling author of *A Dog Named Christmas*

Illustrated by Alessia Girasole

4U2B BOOKS & MEDIA

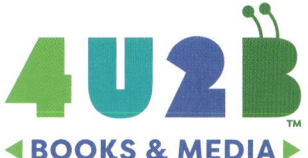

Todd and Laura McCray ran the animal shelter in Crossing Trails, Kansas. They took care of lost and abandoned animals in need of homes.

Their pet of many years, a dog named Christmas, came to work with them every day.

Todd's and Laura's daughter, Allie, loved all animals. If Allie wasn't in school, you'd find her at the shelter.

When Dad bathed and groomed the dogs and cats, Allie helped.

When Mom exercised the dogs, Allie helped.

Delivering dinner to the animals was lots of fun. Allie helped.

But by far, Allie's favorite job was giving a name to every critter that lived for a while in the shelter.

One morning when they arrived at the shelter, Allie spotted a cardboard box at the front door. She knew what that meant.

Sure enough, inside the box was a very small, very young puppy, wrapped in a blanket.

Allie scooped him up.
The puppy wagged his tail.

"Hello, Little No Name.
Pleased to meet you."

Throughout the day, Allie carried him in a puppy pouch nestled against her heart. She thought of nothing else but what to name him.

"Little Bit? Snuggles?"

Allie sighed. "Maybe not. Those names will sound silly when you grow bigger."

That afternoon, the popping of firecrackers woke the puppy from his nap.

# Sizzle! Boom!

The puppy buried his nose and shivered. "Don't be afraid," Allie said soothingly. "Today is the Fourth of July. Some people celebrate Independence Day with picnics, loud fireworks, and colorful sparklers.

Hey! Would Sparkles be a good name for you?"

It was time to close the shelter for the day.
Allie looked at the big-eyed furball in the cage.
"Mom. Dad. I don't want to leave him."

"Hmm," said Dad thoughtfully.
"Hmm," said Mom thoughtfully.

"We have a good idea,"
Mom and Dad said in unison.

They took Allie by the hand.
The whole family, plus their new puppy,
piled into their truck and went home.

At dinner, Allie said, "I'm frustrated. I still haven't found the right name for my puppy. I'm going to think about it while I do my chores."

"I water the pumpkin patch every day," Allie explained to the puppy. "By October, the tiny seeds we planted last week will be big pumpkins."

"We carve faces into the pumpkins, and on Halloween we light candles inside them.

Do you like the name Jack? You're cute like a jack-o'-lantern!"

"At night, I scatter berries, seeds, and grain for our hungry turkeys. In November we gather with family and friends on Thanksgiving Day to share a turkey dinner and give thanks for all the good things in our lives."

"This year, I'm going to give thanks for you! But who are you? Gobbler? Sweet Potato?"

"See this old sled? It's been here since the December when Dad adopted Christmas."

"I could name you Nick, after St. Nicholas. He loved giving gifts and helping people. I like giving presents and helping others, too.

Or how about Kris? That's short for Kris Kringle."

"Bringing in the mail makes me think of Valentine's Day when my friends and I give each other cards. I read them over and over because they remind me that I am loved."

"Cupid is a cute name."

It was bedtime.
Allie was disappointed.
"The puppy still doesn't have a name."

"Why don't you sleep on it, Allie?"
said Mom. She gave Allie a kiss.
"That's a good idea," said Dad.
He gave Allie a kiss.

Mom turned out the light. But just as Dad pulled the door nearly shut—

"WAIT! I have the perfect name!"

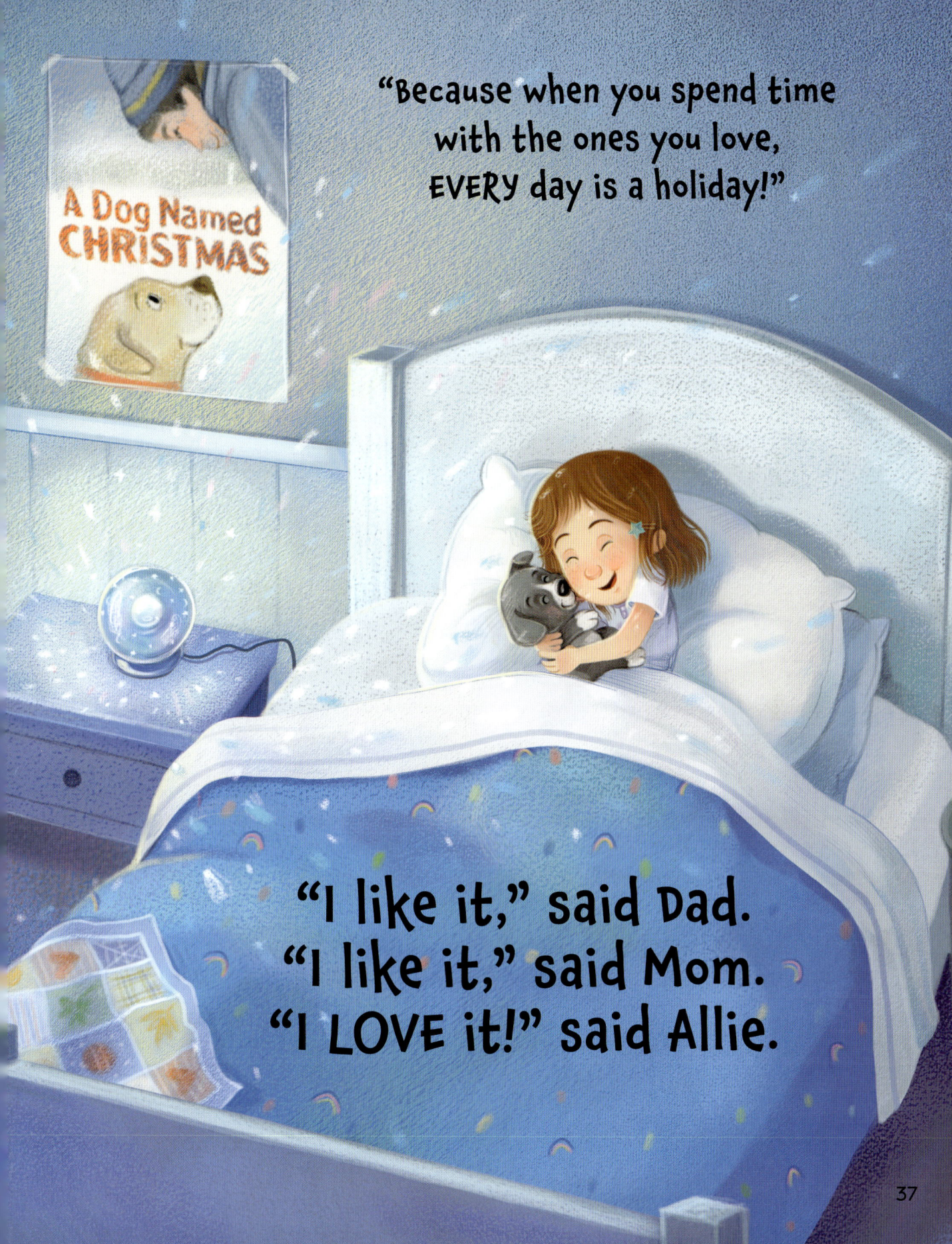

"Because when you spend time with the ones you love, EVERY day is a holiday!"

"I like it," said Dad.
"I like it," said Mom.
"I LOVE it!" said Allie.

# How to Find Your Own Holiday

Visit your nearby shelter or
nonprofit rescue organization.

## QUESTIONS TO ASK:

• Has the animal been spayed or neutered? Microchipped? Vaccinated?

• What resources are available to support our family?

• What do we know about the animal's age, background, temperament, talents, and dislikes?

• What animal will best integrate into our family's lifestyle?

Text Copyright © 2025 Greg Kincaid
Cover art & interior illustrations © 2025 4U2B Books & Media

Illustrator: Alessia Girasole
All rights reserved.

ISBN: 978-0-8294-5699-8
Library of Congress Control Number: 2024940458

Published in Chicago, IL
Printed in China
24 25 26 27 28 29 30 31 32 33 Dream Colour 10 9 8 7 6 5 4 3 2 1